# Doggy Slippers

Poems by **Jorge Luján**
(with the contribution of
Latin American children)

Translated by **Elisa Amado**

Pictures by **Isol**

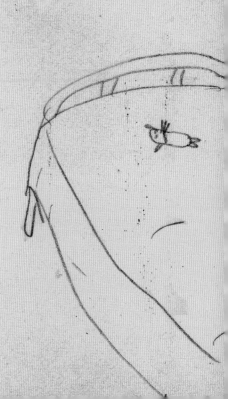

Groundwood Books / House of Anansi Press
Toronto  Berkeley

Groundwood Books / House of Anansi Press
110 Spadina Avenue, Suite 801, Toronto, Ontario M5V 2K4
or c/o Publishers Group West
1700 Fourth Street, Berkeley, CA 94710

We acknowledge for their financial support of our
publishing program the Canada Council for the Arts,
the Government of Canada through the Canada Book Fund
(CBF) and the Ontario Arts Council.

Canada Council    Conseil des Arts
for the Arts      du Canada

ONTARIO ARTS COUNCIL
CONSEIL DES ARTS DE L'ONTARIO

Library and Archives Canada Cataloguing in Publication

Luján, Jorge
Doggy slippers / Jorge Luján ; Isol, illustrator ; Elisa Amado,
translator.

Poems.
Translation of: Pantuflas de perrito.
ISBN 978-0-88899-983-2

I. Isol   II. Amado, Elisa   III. Title.

PQ7298.22.U43P3513 2010   j861'.64   C2010-900594-5

Printed and bound in China

For my aunt Josefina
and her generous heart. *Jorge*

For Simona and Belinda, feline friends
who know more than they say. *Isol*

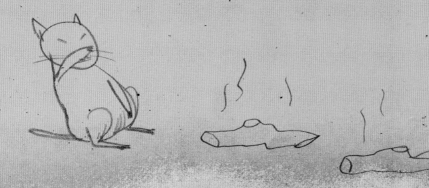

I want to buy
a toy poodle,
a black
girl
puppy
whose name is Olivia.

Do you know where she lives?

My monkey and I are exactly alike
except for our hands and feet,
    our hair,
    our bodies,
    our mouths,
    our clothes,
and that I don't stink.

Littlekins is black, brown and yellow.
When he came he was so small
he fit into my doggy slippers.

He can't remember now
that he was hit by a truck,
or that we put him in a box
with blankets and fresh milk.

Now he's so big
that he doesn't even fit into his name.
And how he howls when the fire truck
siren wails past in the night!

My bunny understands me.
When I'm sad she can tell right away.
And though she walks on four feet
and she likes to bite,
she's nicer than the nicest people.

I
blow
soap
bubbles
and
my
doggie,
Hurricane,
pops
them
with
her
tail.

My turtle, Coco, is happy,
is green,
is slow,
except when she falls
down the stairs.

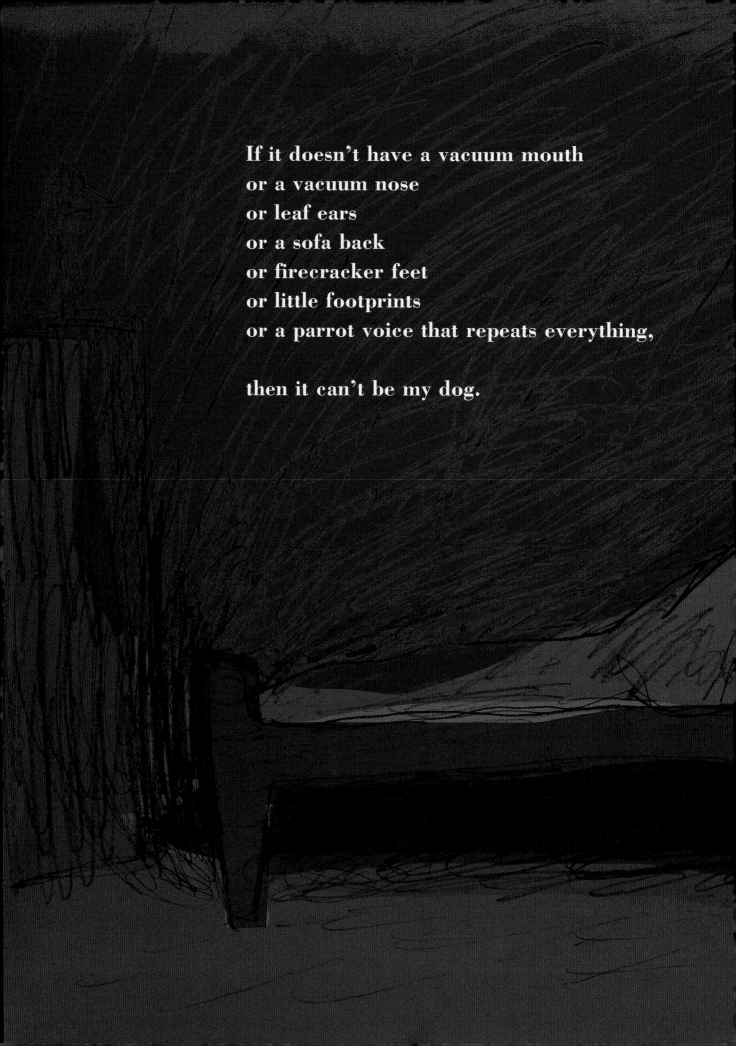

If it doesn't have a vacuum mouth
or a vacuum nose
or leaf ears
or a sofa back
or firecracker feet
or little footprints
or a parrot voice that repeats everything,

then it can't be my dog.

The marmot grrrowls
because he doesn't like
poetry
or his teacher,
who makes him write
nnno-good poems.

Life is good.
Kitty makes it better
when things go wrong.

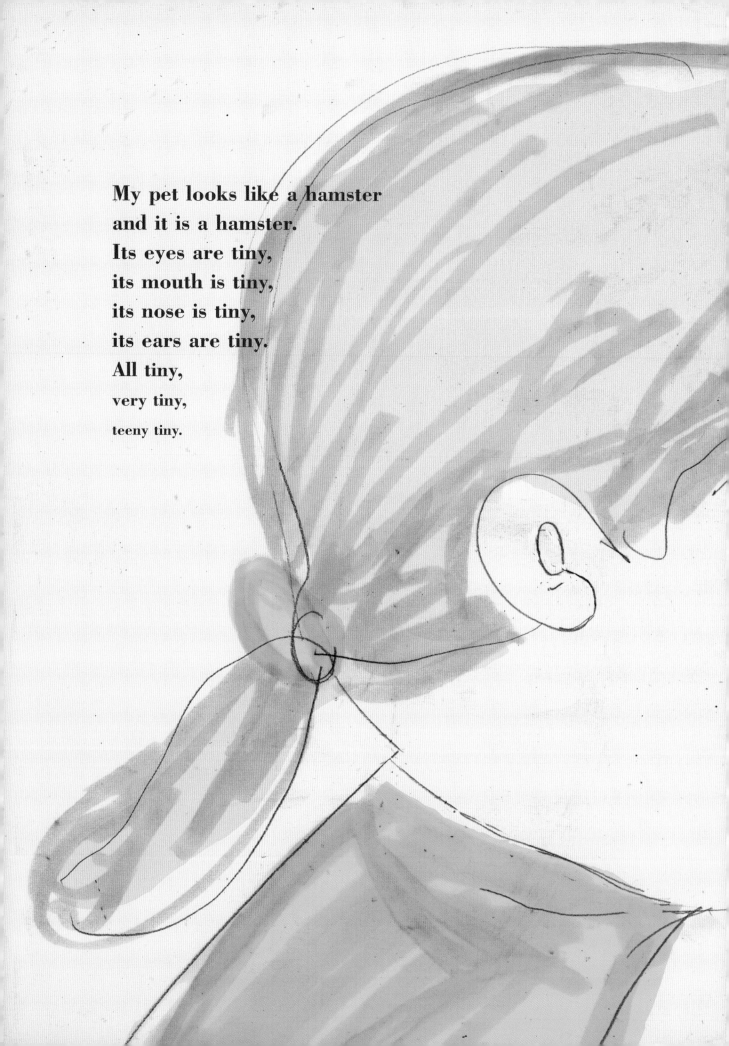

My pet looks like a hamster
and it is a hamster.
Its eyes are tiny,
its mouth is tiny,
its nose is tiny,
its ears are tiny.
All tiny,
very tiny,
teeny tiny.

The
parakeet
talks
and eats his seeds.

That's
his
way
of making life sweet.

On two feet
it's a tightrope-walker.

On four feet
it's a tail-wagger.

On no feet
it's a pillow.

Can you guess…
or do you give up?

*Doggy Slippers* was written with the help of

Azul Smith Johnson (9, Guadalupe, Nuevo León, México)
Clarisa Martínez Lima (7, Buenos Aires, Argentina)
Daniela Martínez Hernández (10, Monterrey, México)
Francisco Elliot Gallegos Mendoza (12, México City, México)
Jesús Salvador Malo Estrella (8, México City, México)
Jorge Eduardo Hersch González (9, México City, México)
María del Carmen Vega Martínez (13, Aguascalientes, México)
Mauricio Pérez Hernández (9, México City, México)
Miguel Ángel Reyes Carvajal (12, México City, México)
Sebastián García Herrera (5, México City, México)
Sol Valeska Ceballos Riebel (9, Ushuaia, Argentina).

To them, and to the almost one hundred children who wrote to
us, our delighted gratitude.

This book was born from a surprising suggestion by Marina Kriscautzky and Miriam Martínez of www.chicosyescritores.com. The idea was to write a collection of poems with the help of children from all over Latin America using the Internet. I should propose a theme, the children would suggest stories, and together we would "cook up" poetry in a kind of poetic kitchen. At the time I didn't imagine that I would be starting on an unforgettable human and creative process, or that one day a wonderful book would come about thanks to the enthusiasm and talent of Isol, my collaborator on so many projects. Jorge Luján